Dear Parents,

Welcome to the Scholastic Reader series. We have taken over 80 years of experience with teachers, parents, and children and put it into a program that is designed to match your child's interests and skills.

Level 1—Short sentences and stories made up of words kids can sound out using their phonics skills and words that are important to remember.

Level 2—Longer sentences and stories with words kids need to know and new "big" words that they will want to know.

Level 3—From sentences to paragraphs to longer stories, these books have large "chunks" of texts and are made up of a rich vocabulary.

Level 4—First chapter books with more words and fewer pictures.

It is important that children learn to read well enough to succeed in school and beyond. Here are ideas for reading this book with your child:

- Look at the book together. Encourage your child to read the title and make a prediction about the story.
- Read the book together. Encourage your child to sound out words when appropriate. When your child struggles, you can help by providing the word.
- Encourage your child to retell the story. This is a great way to check for comprehension.
- Have your child take the fluency test on the last page to check progress.

Scholastic Readers are designed to support your child's efforts to learn how to read at every age and every stage. Enjoy helping your child learn to read and love to read.

—**Francie Alexander**
  Chief Education Officer
  Scholastic Education

Copyright © 1994 by Nancy Hall, Inc.

Fluency activities copyright © 2003 Scholastic Inc.

All rights reserved. Published by Scholastic Inc.
SCHOLASTIC, CARTWHEEL BOOKS, and associated logos are trademarks
and/or registered trademarks of Scholastic Inc.

Library of Congress Cataloging-in-Publication Data is available.

ISBN 0-439-59417-0

10 9 8 7 6 5 4 3 2 1   03 04 05 06 07
Printed in the U.S.A.   23
First printing, November 1994

Bubble Trouble

by Mary Packard
Illustrated by Elena Kucharik

Scholastic Reader — Level 1

Cartwheel
·B·O·O·K·S·®

SCHOLASTIC INC.
New York Toronto London Auckland Sydney
Mexico City New Delhi Hong Kong Buenos Aires

I make bubbles in the air.

I make bubbles in my hair.

I make bubbles big and
round...

and listen for the popping
sound.

See the bubbles in the sink.

Hear the bubbles in my drink.

I make bubbles here

and there.

I make bubbles everywhere!

Here's a bubble.

There's a bubble.

Sorry, Mom.

Am I in trouble?

Rhyme Time

Rhyming words sound alike. Point to the words that rhyme with each other.

drink	sound
hair	bubble
my	sink
round	there
trouble	I

What Happens Next?

At the end of this story, the boy's mother sees all of the bubbles he has made.

How do you think his mother feels about the bubbles? Why do you think that?

What do you think happens next in the story?

Inside Story

Some words have smaller words in them. In each row, you can use your fingers to cover a letter or letters in the first word and make it look like the second word.

hair   air

sink   in

there   here

make   a

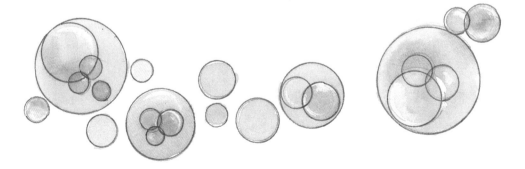

Big Bubbles

These children are blowing bubbles. The boy made a big bubble.

Point to two bubbles that are bigger.

Now point to the bubble that is the biggest.

Starting Off

In each row, point to the word that begins with the same letter as the first word in the row.

sink   see   in   round

make   here   my   for

big   sound bubble air

hair   for and here

there   trouble sink drink

Spring Cleaning

Emily is going to fill a bucket with soap bubbles to wash her bike.

Point to the things she would use.

Then point to the things she would not use.

Answers

(Rhyme Time)

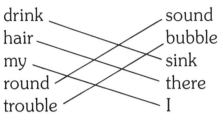

drink — sink
hair — there
my — bubble
round — I
trouble — sound

(What Happens Next?) Answers will vary.

(Inside Story)

h **air**   **air**
s **in** k   **in**
t **here**   **here**
m **a** k e   **a**

(Big Bubbles)

bigger:    biggest:

(Starting Off)

sink   **see** in round
make   here **my** for
big   sound **bubble** air
hair   for and **here**
there   **trouble** sink drink

(Spring Cleaning)

She would use: 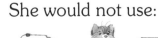   She would not use: